Into The Serpent's Jaws

A JOURNEY OF TRANSFORMATION

Spark Deeley

This is the story of an epic journey made by the spirit through unknown territory.

It encourages us to embrace the darkness, allowing our fears to become our allies.

It is dedicated to all those who walk the path of transformation.

She came bravely through the jungle, in awe of all its life and power and sensing its savageness. She came to know its Darkness ~ the hollows, the marshes and bogs. And she came to know its Light ~ the sun filtering through the trees and the butterfly shimmering every colour imaginable.

She felt there was no place inside the wilderness of herself that she did not know. She had dug through the clay deeper and deeper into what she felt to be the very core of her being. Her hands emerged scratched, her mind weary, her limbs aching. But always she continued, pulled forward into greater depths, knowing that beyond there was greater light.

Then one day there came a place in the jungle that she did not recognize. She did not know the way forward and there was no way back. There was no light above or beyond and all that remained was the stench of decay and the weight of terror.

And so she lay down upon the jungle floor in exhaustion. She wanted to cry, but in her absolute exhaustion she could not.

The earth offered to take her body. Rats sniffed and chattered and a jaguar watched from the limbs of a tree .... waiting .... waiting for the moment when it might take her too.

$\mathcal{A}$ Serpent slithered across her body....

....It opened its jaws wide and started to swallow. It began at her feet and worked up her legs, over her knees and her thighs. It opened wider to accommodate her hips and her belly, sucking at her soft skin, her shoulders, her arms and strong hands. From some distant place inside herself she felt the jaws of the serpent around her neck.

Now there seemed to be no way to save herself, her fear and exhaustion preventing her from moving a muscle.

But the jaws of the serpent did not close around her neck. They widened to take in her head and closed softly around her skull, so that just her face was peeping out from the serpent's mouth. Its teeth glittered like beads of moisture dripping from the forest canopy.

She looked down and saw herself
encased in a jewelled body of turquoise,
red and gold. She made a slight movement
and a ripple ran through her scales. A new
strength trembled inside her as she lifted her
head, which rose up a few stately inches.
With trepidation she looked around her.

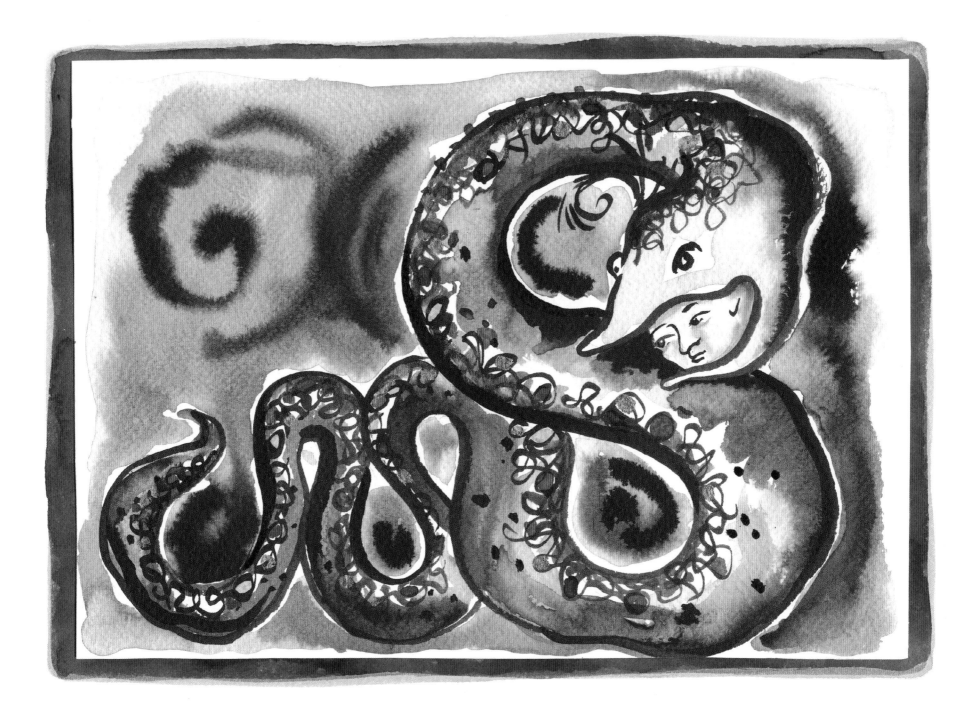

The jaguar snoozed silently above her in the tree. It lazily opened one eye and in that instant an understanding was formed. Now it acknowledged the power of the serpent's protection.

Cautiously, the jaguar inched its way along the branch of the tree, gracefully sprang to the ground and arrived to stare the snakewoman in the face.

Safely encased in the serpent's skin, the woman was somehow no longer afraid. She met the jaguar's gaze without the blink of an eye. After some consideration the jaguar eased itself down upon the damp jungle floor and the snakewoman curled up in its deep fur coat.

The jaguar's fur was soft and sumptuous. Warmth from its body seeped through the cool surface of the serpent's skin and into the woman within.

With her two extra skins she felt safe at last, and she rested.

As she slept ancient memories filtered
through her body. They seemed to have been
formed in a time long before her existence and
yet were stored deep within her bones. As
they loosened they merged with the beat of
her heart. She was brought to consciousness with a
startling clarity that made her call out into the night.

All this at a time when her exhaustion was
so deep, she was unable to shed a tear.

Days passed, weeks even, she drank a drop of water occasionally from the tips of the jungle leaves. The jaguar fed her with jungle fruits as they dropped from the jungle bushes. And very gradually the woman began to regain her strength.

However there were still days when she could barely lift her head and others when she could only curl up small, hidden from the world in the dark folds of the jaguar's pelt.

And yet there were times when she left the safety of the luxurious fur and moved silently around the jungle, navigating its darkness with more certainty and confronting her fears of its savageness anew.

For now that she was a part of the jungle, she was also a part of its power.

And she knew that in some way it had claimed her, just as she had agreed to surrender herself to its teachings.

As Winter passed, the light of Spring came and then the heat of Summer. The jaguar still lived close by in the trees and gently the serpent also made it clear that it was time for the woman to move out of the protection of its jewelled skin.

Little by little, not only did she begin to edge herself outwards, but the serpent began the process of expelling her.

Her body was different from having been contained in the serpent's skin for so long. The soft furry protection of the jaguar's pelt was also gone.

She felt naked in a way that she had never done before. Even the tickle of a butterfly alighting on her skin felt almost too much to bear. She found tears releasing at the tiniest scratch from a thorn and she felt heat and cold with more intensity. And yet . . . .

... She also felt love with a more open and tender heart.

And an unshakable wholeness in what she now knew to be the very core of her being.

She was home at last.

The quetzal birds screeched above her with delight at her emergence. For now she shared the power and knowledge of the darkest corners of the jungle, and there was no place left inside her to fear.